Praise for *A Gift of Christmas Song*

"*A Gift of Christmas Song* will have you yearning to sit by a crackling fire sipping a warm cup of spiced cider tea on a cool winter night. Laura's writing captures the true essence of Christmas and the love that's possible when barriers are dropped and hearts are opened. This book is truly a gift!"

> –Sage Lewis, author of *JAVA: The True Story* and *Where Angels Play: Life, Death and the Magic Beyond*– www.DancingPorcupine.com

"*A Gift of Christmas Song* reads like a song in itself, soothing the soul and lifting the heart as only Laura can do."

> –Connie Grauds, author of *Jungle Medicine* and *Amazon Speaks*–www.conniegrauds.com

"*A Gift of Christmas Song* is a tender story that reminds us of the power of song to open the heart, call forth magic, and connect people to each other. It is a perfect thing to read in deep winter, perhaps out loud to a beloved companion. With cocoa, of course."

> –Barbara McAfee, singer, songwriter,voice coach, and author of *Full Voice: The Art and Practice of Vocal Presence*– www.barbaramcafee.com

"This richly resonant book is the best present ever! It will make your heart sing, make your eyes tear up, and warm your Christmas like a hot cup of cocoa in a storm. With *A Gift of Christmas Song*, Laura D'Ambrosio inspires peace, kindness, compassion, and joy with her skillful, heartfelt storytelling."

> –Lynn Baskfield, SpiritDance coaching, author of *Some People You Will Always Love: Finding the Stories that Satisfy Your Soul*–www.equinecoaching.com

★

A Gift
of
Christmas
Song

A Gift
of
Christmas Song

Laura D'Ambrosio

www.lauradambrosio.com

Library of Congress Cataloging-in-Publication Data has been applied for.

ISBN: 978-0-9971335-2-3

10 9 8 7 6 5 4 3 2 1

For the song inside of everyone and everything

A GIFT
of
CHRISTMAS
SONG

★

At the Johnsons', all was not calm and bright. It was tense. Twelve-year-old Sam was doing his best to avoid his mom and dad, holed up in his room with the door closed. He'd created a family storm after he'd announced he was quitting the St. Paul Children's Choir, right before the big Christmas Eve concert. His dad, Jim, was angry and took Sam's cell phone as punishment. His mom, Sarah, pleaded with him to tell her what was wrong, but Sam clammed up and refused to talk.

While Sam fumed, a winter storm roared in from the northwest, collecting strength as it crossed the Dakota plains, slammed into Minnesota, and crossed the river to batter Wisconsin. Snow fell fast in the little town along the river where Sam lived. Fierce winds drove snow into wild drifts, and the roads quickly became undriveable. Plunging temperatures encased tree limbs and powerlines in a heavy sheath of ice. One event after another canceled, including the concert Sam was supposed to sing in.

Sam tiptoed into the kitchen, avoiding his parents. As he opened the refrigerator, the power failed, silencing the appliances, and plunging the house into darkness. Outside the neighborhood Christmas lights blinked out in chorus, casting Santa and his reindeer into shadowy silhouettes and leaving the baby Jesus in a dark manager. Once-bright windows went black, like a curtain dropped unexpectedly on the Christmas pageant.

Sam heard his mom rummage in the junk drawer. She called out to his dad, "Where are the flashlights?" Just as suddenly as it went off, the power came back on, and Sam heard the buzz of the generator his dad had bought last year, despite his mom's protests. His dad thumped up from the basement, pleased with himself. "At least one family in this town has power," he said flopping onto a kitchen chair. His mom shut the drawer and put her hands on her hips, like she was going to argue, but instead dropped her arms and said, "I suppose it's a good thing. I checked the weather. It's a big storm."

Sam walked to the living room and joined his sister at the window. He pressed his nose against the cold glass and peered at the dark house across the street. "It looks lonely with no lights," Sandy said. "Is that lady ok, dad?"

His dad shrugged. "They'll get the power on soon. Storm's expected to die down by evening. She'll be ok."

"The old lady's probably doing something creepy in the dark." Sam cackled. "My buddy Franklin says she's a witch."

His mom shot him a reproachful look as her phone chimed with an incoming text. She held the phone up. "Good news! The concert's still canceled, but the director heard that the plows should clear our streets tonight. All the kids who live nearby are going to sing at the church tonight." She looked hopefully at Sam. "They'd love to have you join them…"

Sam rolled his eyes and jerked his head at the

window. "You can't sing a duet by yourself. Angie lives in Minnetonka, like hours from here."

His mom bit her lip as his dad slapped the table. "What's wrong with you?" his dad growled. "All this time schlepping you to practice, and you just quit?"

Sam balled his fists. "I told you already."

He ran up the stairs into his room, slammed the door, and paced like a caged animal, wanting to be anywhere but home. As his dad banged on his bedroom door, Sam held his breath. He heard his mom say, "Just let him be." Relieved, he let out his breath and leaned on the window ledge.

Outside, the wind calmed, then roared. He shivered and felt like there was a storm inside his stomach. He glanced out at the dark houses, wondering what other people were doing without a generator; people like the old woman he'd made fun of earlier. Sam rubbed a spot on the cold glass to clear the fog and thought he saw faint light in one of the windows of her house. "Probably chanting in front of a fire," Sam thought and threw himself on his bed.

n the house across the street, Marie Andraski relaxed into her couch, cradling a glass of rich red wine and listening to the storm beat a rhythm with the crackle and pop of the fire. Tapered candles and a cheery fire cast flickering light and warmth into her dark home. She noticed the only house on the street with power was the Johnsons'.

"They seem like a nice family," she said aloud to herself. But this past autumn, the Johnson boy and his pack of friends had taunted her as she raked leaves, calling her an old witch, shoving each other, and running off, laughing. Thinking about it now, she chuckled. The boys reminded her of hyena packs she'd seen while on safari. The thought made her smile. She assumed they'd grow out of it…eventually.

On this wintery night, Marie was acutely aware how little she knew her neighbors. But that was by choice. She went out of her way to be as inconspicuous as possible because, in another life far from this small town, the world knew her as Marie Anders, whose last concert with the Chicago Philharmonic had won the Grammy for Best Classical Performance, an award she'd added to other genre-crossing awards in jazz and pop.

She tossed another log on the fire and remembered the last time she sang onstage. It was three years ago, Christmas Eve. Closing her eyes, Marie could still see Sophie standing backstage, one hand on her heart and the other blowing a kiss. Such joy in those moments. They didn't know that two days later, Sophie would be diagnosed with a fast moving, incurable lymphoma.

Marie raised her glass. "Sophie, it's Christmas Eve, and a silent night without power…I miss you." She took a sip and, taking a deep, slow breath, she reached for how it felt to sing – that exhilarating mix of fear and elation when she gave herself completely to the song. It was magical. "It's as if songs fly throughout the universe," she told *The Globe* during an interview. "Sometimes they choose me. I don't sing the song; the song sings me."

When Marie sang, she gave audiences the illusion of intimacy, but her true intimacy was reserved for Sophie. Now, as she heard the winds begin to calm, she wrapped her sweater tight, like a hug, and murmured, "I can't sing for anyone anymore, Sophie. Without you, the magic is…gone."

Sophie was her best friend, her partner, her confidant, her muse. The two happily orbited their private world for decades. For weeks after Sophie died, people called with condolences and food often arrived unannounced, but that eventually faded, and Marie realized she had no one to talk with except her therapist, and that was not the same as a friend.

One windy, cold, grey day, as she vainly attempted to hail a cab during the Chicago rush hour, she remembered walking with Sophie along a path next to the St. Croix River in a little town north of Minneapolis. The B&B they had stayed in was an older house with a generous kitchen and a comfortable living room with a large fireplace surrounded by river stones. Bees and birds hovered in the beautiful native plantings in the front yard, while the back was shaded by towering pine trees.

When she got home, she looked up the B&B and found it was for sale. Marie sold her condo, bought the old B&B, and turned it into a warm, welcoming, home; her sanctuary in the Northwoods. She kept to herself, ordered most things online, and avoided face-to-face conversation. The last thing she wanted for anyone to know where Marie Anders had disappeared to. People were nice but mostly left her alone, which was exactly what she wanted.

Outside, the winds slowed as the powerful storm sped southeast. In its wake, stars appeared, and a cold stillness settled over the town. Marie sipped her wine, watched the fire, began to hum "Silent Night," then sighed.

★

cross the street from Marie, Sam half-heartedly rolled a ball to make snowman while his dad shoveled. He wore snow pants, boots, and mittens but, like most 12-year-old boys, he left his jacket unzipped despite the cold. He grabbed his sister's arm. "Let's go spy on the old lady."

"I don't want to." Sandy tried to pull her arm free.

"Fine…you're a baby anyway." Sam let go, and she tumbled into a deep drift.

Jim stopped his shoveling. "Leave your sister alone. You're in enough hot water." He marched over to Sam, glowering, handed him the shovel, and helped Sandy up.

Sam threw the shovel on the walk and took off across the road, "Christmas sucks! Singing sucks! You suck. I'm out of here."

"Sam, get back here! Sam!"

Sam ignored his dad and pushed his legs through snowdrifts until he was behind the neighbor's houses across the street and out of his dad's sight. Breathing hard, he leaned against a tall pine tree, brushing a branch that dropped a load of snow down his back. Punching the tree in frustration, he saw that he was behind Marie's house. Maybe he could prove she was a real witch, he thought, or at least have an adventure he could brag about to Franklin and his other friends.

There was a juniper hedge under the window. Sam snuck up then tamped the snow to the left of the window into a ledge strong enough to hold his weight. He clambered up, one hand on the casing to balance as he bent to peer inside.

The same moment Sam leaned sideways and tilted his head to look inside, Marie leaned forward to look outside to see what the storm had done to her trees. Inches from each other, their eyes locked. Marie screamed, and Sam toppled off his snowy perch and landed face down in the juniper hedge. Marie saw Sam's feet framed in her window.

"Oh, good grief," Marie muttered as she threaded her feet into her boots, hurriedly tossed on a down jacket, mittens, and a wool hat, and waded through the drifts to where Sam struggled in the hedge. She grabbed the back of his pants and yanked him out like a momma dog grabbing a misbehaving puppy by the scruff. Sam sprawled, snow-covered, on the drift, snow melting down his back.

"Well, go on home then. You had your fun." Marie turned to slog back to her door.

"I'm not going home," Sam muttered, shaking snow from his hair, not daring to look at her.

Marie stopped. "Really? On Christmas Eve. Where are you off to, then?"

"Anywhere but there." Sam struggled to right himself.

"Ah, running away," Marie said, studying the young boy with interest now. "I know something about that," she whispered softly to herself. Seeing a snow-covered Sam still knee deep in the snow, Marie made a choice. "Well, you can't run away with wet clothes. You can come in and dry off, then be on your way." She swept her arm towards the door.

Sam glared at her. He tried to brush the snow off his head and shoulders, but more crept behind his coat. The last thing he wanted was to hang out with her, but he was getting cold and the idea of going home to face his parents was worse than the thought of getting warm inside this old lady's house, so he followed her to the door.

nside, Sam kicked off his boots, dropped his soggy mittens, and peeled off his wet snow pants. His jeans were mostly dry, but his sweatshirt was soaked. Marie hung her jacket on a hook and placed her boots on a plastic tray. She pointed to the other hook, and Sam hung his jacket there. She waited. Sam got the hint and placed his boots next to hers. "Thank you," Marie said.

She pulled a fleece blanket from a bin. "I'm going to get you a shirt to change into." Marie handed the blanket to Sam, then taking the flashlight she'd left by the door, she headed down the hall.

He hung his wet sweatshirt on the last hook, pulled the fleece over his shoulders, and cautiously walked into the living room. What he saw surprised him. He didn't know what he'd expected, but he hadn't imagined the old lady would have artwork that looked like real paintings and what looked like a small grand piano. The place felt almost magical in the flickering candlelight.

Sam slowly wandered the room, taking it in. He stopped in front of shelf that held a few gold trophies that looked familiar. Leaning in, he read the words: "National Academy of Recording Arts & Sciences MARIE ANDERS Best Classical Vocal Performance." He gasped. There were two more, one for Best Pop Vocal Performance and another for Best Jazz Vocal Album. Looking over his shoulder to make sure Marie wasn't there, Sam grabbed one of the Grammy Awards trophies, stepped back and held it high, imagining he was on the stage receiving the award himself.

"Heavier than they look, aren't they?" Marie's amused voice startled Sam and he replaced the Grammy with a thump.

"I'm…I'm sorry." Sam said.

"It's fine," she said.

Sam's mouth hung open.

"Not the old witch you expected, am I?" Marie said, handing him a faded University of Illinois sweatshirt. Grateful for old gas stoves that worked even when the power was out, she placed two mugs of hot cocoa on the table in front of the fireplace.

Sam dropped the fleece and shrugged into the sweatshirt.

Marie was surprised to feel pleased to see someone wearing Sophie's old favorite. "It fits you." She paused. "It was my partner Sophie's favorite."

"Did you guys break up or something?" Sam blurted.

Marie surprised herself again by laughing. "No, she died."

Sam looked away.

Marie settled into a chair and indicated the couch. "Drink your hot cocoa, and let's hear why you're running away."

Sam sat, sipped the sweet chocolate, and remembered he was angry. "Christmas sucks. Mom and Dad suck. So does that stupid choir. I told them I'm done singing."

Marie nodded. "Christmas can be annoying. Too much fake cheer if you ask me. And parents can be a pain. I could tell you stories." She chuckled. "But I don't get why you lump singing in the same category. Why stop singing?"

"It's stupid. Only babies sing in choirs. I've got better things to do," Sam said, his voice thick.

"Oh, yeah? Like throw snowballs at my house with your pack of hyena friends?"

"We were just messing around!"

"Right." Marie waited as Sam grew quiet.

What he'd never told anyone was that when he'd tried to tell his friends about how he felt when he sang, they made fun of him. Taunted him. Especially Franklin. Franklin had told him he was a baby. He laughed at him and even called him a weirdo. Sam fought back at first, but his desire to part of the pack was overwhelming, so he'd quit the choir and stopped singing. But when he was alone, his stomach hurt when he thought he'd never sing again.

Sam placed the empty mug on the table, looked fiercely at Marie, and said, "I've heard about you. You used to be famous. Then you stopped singing."

Taken aback, Marie starred at Sam. "I did," she nodded. "In public." She fell still for a moment, and then continued: "I still sing though, because I can't *not* sing. The songs ask me, need me." She gestured to the photos of her and Sophie on the mantle. "So, I sing for Sophie."

Sam sat straight up, his body alert. He'd never heard anyone talk about music in that way. That's what he'd tried to explain to his buddieshow he felt that he didn't sing the song–the song sang him.

"What were you supposed to sing at the concert?" she asked.

" 'O Holy Night' was supposed to be a solo, and the duet was 'The Prayer.' "

"Ah, 'The Prayer.' Andrea Bocelli and Céline Dion made that song famous. Are you singing the Italian or the English part?"

"Uh, we both were singing in English," Sam said. Then he got up and paced in front of the fireplace. "Why do you care? I'm not singing in the concert. Mom and Dad hate me. My choir hates me. My friends think I'm a weirdo. Everything sucks." He slumped back into the couch and put his head in his hands.

arie watched the flames slowly dance in the fireplace, thought of Sophie, squared her shoulders, and took a deep breath. "Sam, I haven't sung for another person in over two years, but I'll make you a deal: I'll sing if you will."

Sam dropped his hands, astonished, and looked up. "Right now?"

"Right now. No criticism. Just singing." Straightening her spine, Marie tilted her head. She sang softly with her eyes closed:

> *Silent night, holy night*
> *All is calm, all is bright*
> *Round yon virgin mother and child*
> *Holy infant so tender and mild*
> *Sleep in heavenly peace*
> *Sleep in heavenly peace*

Marie felt the song descend from far away and the familiar butterflies in her belly, a warning from her ego that it did not like giving up control to the music. She relaxed, invited the song in, and became one with the music. She could never adequately explain the mix of euphoria and fear; the sheer awesomeness of how this felt. As she sang the last notes, she felt the music loosen the knot of grief that held her captive. A spark of peace kindled deep within her heart. Tears gathered as she opened her eyes and looked at Sam.

Sam felt like he'd just discovered a gift under the tree: one that he hadn't asked for, but it turned out to be the best present of his whole Christmas. He didn't know how to explain it, so he sang.

O Holy Night!

The stars are brightly shining

It is the night of the dear Savior's birth!

Long lay the world in sin and error pining

Till he appeared, and the soul felt its worth.

A thrill of hope the weary soul rejoices

For yonder breaks a new and glorious morn!

Fall on your knees

Oh hear the angel voices

Oh night divine

Oh night when Christ was born

Oh night divine

Oh night divine

As he sang, Sam's body relaxed, his face released the scowl he'd adapted to look cool, and he let the music flow through him. When he hit the high note—*oh night divine*—he felt as though his heart would explode. When finished, he looked shyly at

Marie and said, "The song sings me. That's what made Franklin and the others laugh at me. But it does."

Marie could only nod as she wept.

Sam was surprised as tears flowed like a flood. He folded his arms, dropped his head, and let go. When the flood became a trickle and then stopped, he felt like all the painful stuff he'd been feeling the past few weeks was washed away. He didn't feel funny crying in front of Marie, but he kept his head down, unsure.

"You have a gift," Marie told him, drying her eyes. "Not only because you have a beautiful voice. It's because you *feel* the music. You sense when it chooses you, and you allow it to happen." Sam felt the truth in her words, slowly raised his head and, without looking directly at Marie, softly said, "They canceled the concert in the Twin Cities because of the storm, but the kids who live around here are going to sing at the church tonight."

Marie, aware how tender this moment was, paused, then gently asked, "Do you want to sing with them now?"

"Yeah, but they'll think I'm nuts." Sam sighed. "Maybe they don't want me." His voice cracked with emotion.

"They might think you're nuts," Marie smiled. "But I'm guessing they'll be happy to have you back." She felt Sam's enthusiasm and his hesitation. Encouraging him, she asked, "Is the singer you're doing the duet with going to be there?"

Sam shook his head. "She lives in Minnetonka. No way she's getting here. But I can sing with the choir and do my solo."

Marie placed another log on the fire and glanced at the clock on the mantle. "When is the concert?"

"In less than an hour."

"I have an idea." Sam scowled. Marie took a deep breath and said, "How about I sing with you?"

Sam's jaw dropped. "Really?" he said. Marie nodded.

"That would be awesome!" Sam couldn't believe it.

Marie pointed at the clock. "We don't have much time to practice. I can sing either part in English or Italian. You chose."

Sam thought for a second and then decided: "It would be cool if you sang the Italian part that Andrea Bocelli sings."

Marie clapped her hands. "*Bellissima*! Very beautiful. I believe you have the first verse."

The candlelight danced across the frosted windows as Marie listened to Sam sing the first verse. Marie was thrilled at how good Sam was. Young, but good. He reminded her of herself almost 50 years ago. How she wished Sophie were there to hear him!

As Sam sang, his body felt warm, not just from the fire keeping the old house warm despite no power, but from inside out, like singing was a flame burning inside his chest. When Marie sang her part, he thought it was so cool how easily her voice blended with his and he knew enough to realize how incredible she was.

When they finished, Sam grinned at Marie. "Wow," he said.

She nodded then twirled her finger. "Again."

They rehearsed as much as they could until it was time to go.

As Sam slipped his boots on, he asked Marie if he could give her the sweatshirt back the next day. "Keep it," Marie said, knowing Sophie would be pleased.

Sam opened the door then froze. "I forgot. My folks don't know where I've been."

"It's okay. I texted them when I made the hot chocolate and told them you had run away and landed in my shrubs. They were upset, but at least they know you weren't frozen in a drift somewhere."

"They're still going to, like, ground me for a month."

Marie gave him a gentle prod to get him moving, then shut the door behind them.

am led the way across the freshly plowed street to his house, his stomach in a knot. He was relieved that his mom and dad knew where he was, but he didn't want to face them. The warm, golden light of the only house with power spilled onto the freshly shoveled driveway. He squared his shoulders and opened the door. His mom rushed into the foyer and hugged him. He squirmed a little but hugged her back.

"I'm sorry, Mom," he said. He looked over his mom's shoulder and saw his dad planted with arms folded. "I'm sorry, Dad."

"We were worried, kiddo," his dad said gruffly.

Marie cleared her throat and Sam spun around. "Uh, mom, you know Marie. And um, well, I decided to sing tonight. And um, Marie's gonna come too."

His mom and dad shared a surprised look. His dad opened his mouth but before he could say anything, his mom said, "Well, let's get going then. We don't have much time to get there."

His dad turned. "I'll start the truck. Come on, Sandy. Get your coat."

Marie waited on the front steps while Sarah locked the front door. "That's one incredible young man," she told Sarah. They watched Sam waiting for them, jumping up and down, unable to contain his energy. Sarah took Marie's mittened hand in hers and squeezed, her eyes saying thank you.

They piled in the truck, Sandy squished between Sam and Marie in the back seat.

The freshly plowed church parking lot held more cars than Sam expected to see as his dad nosed into a spot. His stomach tingled with excitement.

Sam left the others at the entrance to the church and slid in the side door where the choir kids were gathered around Mr. Vargus, their director. As he walked towards the group, the chatter stopped.

Sam took a deep breath, looked the director in the eye and announced: "I know I've been jerk and I let you down. I'm sorry. I'm here to sing if you'll let me."

The director studied Sam for a moment, then nodded. "Are you ready to sing your solo?"

"I am, sir."

"What do you think, kids?"

Sam felt his stomach unclench as heads nodded and most of the kids said yes.

Peeking inside the church, Sam saw Franklin and some of the guys in the pews. They looked unhappy, like they'd been dragged there by their parents. He was surprised that he felt nothing; no fear about what they would say or do. It was like he now lived in a different world.

Though shrunk in size by the storm, the choir sang with gusto. The whole time, Sam felt like he was flying on currents of music. When he sang his solo, he felt like he was soaring like a hawk over a river.

fter the last song, the audience applauded enthusiastically. Sam left his spot and approached the director. "I didn't have time to tell you before the concert, I'm singing the duet." He paused and motioned to the center aisle to Marie as she walked towards them. "With a special guest."

Those who had begun to gather their hats and mittens stopped and watched as Marie confidently strode onto the little stage as if it were Carnegie Hall.

"Mr. Vargus," Sam said, "this is Marie. She's singing with me."

Marie offered her hand to the director, in part to steady the man who looked stunned to find a famous singer in the little church. "Thank you for allowing me to sing with Sam tonight," she said.

The director found his voice, raised his hands, and announced to the audience, "Please remain seated. We have one more song for you tonight." Then he stepped back to stand with the choir.

Marie and Sam moved to the center of the little stage. The crowd grew silent as people settled. A few people gasped as they realized who Marie was. She nodded at Sam, hummed to give him the opening note, and he began to sing.

As Sam and Marie gave themselves to the song, Marie felt like a host of heavenly angels sang through them, bringing peace to all creatures on earth.

Sam thought that maybe this was how the Grinch felt when he heard the villagers singing and figured out the true meaning of Christmas. Was it love? Sam didn't know for sure, but he knew he wanted to keep singing and feeling this way.

In the pews, people pulled out tissues to dab at suddenly moist eyes. A quarrelling couple reached for each other's hands. An old woman leaned over and said, "I love you, my baby girl." And her daughter laughed because for a moment it was as if Alzheimer's did not exist.

Not one person remained untouched.

As the last notes faded, no one applauded. It was as if they knew any noise would break the spell. They left the church in silence.

he town's power came back on as the Johnsons pulled in the driveway. As Sam's dad ran in to turn off the generator, taking Sandy with him, Sam looked at his footprints in the snow and remembered the run that landed him in Marie's shrubs and onto the stage. He heard his mom and Marie saying goodbye and suddenly didn't want Marie to leave. Not yet.

He looked at his mom and blurted, "Mom, can Marie come in for Christmas cookies?"

"Of course! If she wants to, that is."

"That would be lovely," Marie said and followed Sarah to the house.

Inside, Sam handed Marie a cup of hot cocoa and grabbed a frosted sugar cookie from the plate his mom held. His stomach felt calmer now, and he had a warm feeling in his chest. He figured he was probably still grounded for a month, and he did not want to have "the talk" with his parents, but he felt pretty lucky to have weathered the storm of the past few weeks.

Marie sipped the warm chocolate and settled into the soft couch. She refused a cookie and was only going to stay a short time. This evening had been remarkable, but she wasn't ready to become part of the fabric of the Johnsons' family life.

News of this Christmas Eve duet would spread and, while she wasn't ready to leap back on stage, she thought it might be possible to take one small step. What that step was, she'd decide later.

Acknowledgements

Just as songs choose my character, Marie,
I feel like this story chose me. The story
whooshed in one morning after I read a
daily word posted in the Line-a-Day Writing
Challenge. Line-a-Day is a Skype chat group
of colleagues; a place to share poetry, fiction,
and thoughts prompted by a new word each
day. Thank you, my friends and colleagues,
for your support, encouragement, and
laughter. You make me a better writer.

I am especially grateful to Bethany Snyder,
editor, writing coach, and teacher, who
made this story become so much more than I
imagined. And who taught me the true value
of an editor. I am excited to learn more.

Thanks to my early readers: Sage Lewis,
Heidi Green, Eda Schmidt, Mark

D'Ambrosio, and my mom, Darlene D'Ambrosio. Your insights and questions helped the story become real. And thanks to Jennifer Ingraham for copy editing on Christmas Eve Day!

Thanks to Barbara McAfee, singer/songwriter/performer, who shared how it feels to be sung by the song. She told me that Marie would weep, and she was right.

Finally, deep gratitude to the mystery, the muse, who sweeps in and delivers gifts of unbounded magic.

LISTEN TO THE SONGS

Songs are important part of this story, and I encourage you to listen to how different singers interpret these songs and others. Visit www.lauradambrosio.com for my recommendations.

ABOUT THE AUTHOR

Photo: Kimberly B. Saros

Laura D'Ambrosio designs and writes award-winning training programs, animated videos, and speeches for international corporate clients. As a child, D'Ambrosio always had her nose in a book, and she loved to connect with the people around her through storytelling and music. Now, as an author, she hopes to inspire peace, kindness, compassion, and joy around the world. An avid environmentalist, Laura loves to immerse herself in nature, whether it be camping, taking care of her plants, meditating outdoors, or taking her dog, Teddy, on a hike or walk around the neighborhood. She shares her love of song by singing with a hospice choir. Laura lives in St. Paul, Minnesota, and enjoys spending time with her friends, family, and Teddy.

www.lauradambrosio.com

★